Nick Ford Mysteries

Big Ben is Dead

by
Jerry Stemach

Don Johnston Incorporated
Volo, Illinois

Edited by: Jerry Stemach, MS, CCC-SLP
Speech/Language Pathologist, Director of Content Development, Start-to-Finish ™ Books,

Gail Portnuff Venable, MS, CCC-SLP
Speech/Language Pathologist, San Francisco, California

Dorothy Tyack, MA
Learning Disabilities Specialist, San Francisco, California

Consultant: Ted S. Hasselbring, PhD
William T. Brian Professor of Special Education Technology, University of Kentucky

Copy Editor: Susan Kedzior

Cover Design and Illustrations: Jeff Ham, Karyl Shields

Interior Illustrations: Jeff Ham

Read by: Ed Smaron

Audio Producer: Mark Blottner

Sound Engineer: Tom Krol, *TK Audio Studios*

Published by:

Don Johnston Incorporated
26799 West Commerce Drive
Volo, IL 60073
800.999.4660 USA Canada
800.889.5242 Tech Support
www.donjohnston.com

DON JOHNSTON

International Standard Book Number
ISBN 1-893376-41-9

Contents

A Note from the Start-to-Finish Editors

This book is for my friend,
Chuck Degagne.
Chuck is a farmer
who plants ideas in my head.

Many people have contributed to Big Ben Is Dead.
My wife, Beverly, my daughters, Kristie and Sarah
My friends and colleagues
Gail Portnuff Venable and Dorothy Tyack
Alan Venable
Rachel Whitaker
The entire staff at Don Johnston Incorporated
TK Audio
Kevin Feldman
Michael Benedetti, Michael Sturgeon, Melia Dicker
Robert Berta, photographer
Les and Julie Spencer
and the good people of London.

Chapter 1

The Mummy

"I am so excited to be in England!" said Kris Ford.

"Me, too!" said Mandy Ming. "I can hardly wait to get to London!"

Two boys were standing next to Kris and Mandy. One of the boys was Jeff Ford, who was Kris's brother. The other boy was Ken Rice. Ken Rice was Jeff's best friend. After flying all the way from New York City, the four kids had just landed at Heathrow airport near London.

"I just want to get some sleep," said Ken. "That was a long flight."

Jeff looked at his watch. "I haven't changed my watch yet," he said. "My watch says that it's 6 o'clock in the morning in New York."

"You two boys are not exactly party animals," said Mandy. "Look outside. The sun is shining. It's nearly lunchtime in London," she said. "We have some sightseeing to do before we think about sleeping."

Both boys sat down and moaned. Jeff closed his eyes.

"Where's Nick?" asked Kris. Nick Ford was Kris and Jeff's father.

"Nick must still be in customs," said Mandy. The kids looked behind them and saw Nick Ford. He was standing at a table with a man in a uniform. The man was a customs officer and he was looking through Nick's suitcase. The man took out Nick's laptop computer and set it on the table.

"That customs officer wants to check Nick's computer," said Jeff.

"Why?" asked Mandy.

"Because you can hide a bomb inside a computer," said Ken. "Other people have smuggled bombs into London that way before."

At last, Nick came over to the kids. "I'm sorry that you had to wait," he said. "They wanted to look at my laptop and my camera."

Nick Ford was in London, England, to help some scientists at the British Museum. The scientists had opened up a coffin from Egypt and found a mummy inside. The coffin and the mummy were 3,300 years old.

There were also some seeds inside the coffin. Nick and the scientists wanted to study them to see if such old seeds would still grow.

"We have to find a Tube stop," said Nick.

"I have a tube of toothpaste in my backpack," said Jeff.

Nick laughed. "Not that kind of tube," he said. " 'The Tube' is the name of the underground train here. There's a train station right inside the airport."

Kris pointed at a woman who was standing behind a counter. "Let's ask that lady over there," said Kris. "Maybe she knows about the Tube."

Everyone followed Kris over to the counter. Nick asked the lady if she knew about the train station.

When Nick and the kids got closer to the counter, the lady spoke. "You must be Nick Ford," she said.

"That's right," said Nick.

"How would you and your friends here like some money?" she asked.

Chapter 2

Big Ben is Dead

Ken looked at the lady behind the counter. "Are you giving away money?" he asked her.

The lady smiled. "Well, I'm not exactly giving it away," she answered. "But I am selling it."

"How did you know my name?" asked Nick.

"Because I saw it on your jacket," she said. "It says 'Nick Ford, CCNY.' "

"Oh!" said Nick. "Yes, that's my name all right. The CCNY stands for City College of New York.

I teach biology there." Nick put his arms around Jeff and Kris. "This is my son and my daughter and their two friends," he said. "They are all students at City College."

"It's nice to meet you," said the lady. "Welcome to England. Now, how can I help you?" she asked.

Nick asked about the train station again.

Then Ken spoke. "Why do you want to sell us money?" he asked.

Jeff smiled. "Because our money is no good here," he answered. "They don't use U.S. money in England. But this nice lady will sell us some British money," he said. "You'd better get some if you want to buy anything over here."

Nick and each of the kids exchanged some of their U.S. money for British money and thanked the lady for her help.

It took about 40 minutes to get from the airport to London on the Tube.

There was a long line of cabs waiting at the train station in London.

"These cabs are different from the cabs in New York," sald Krls. "Most of the cabs in New York are yellow and most of these cabs are black."

Nick smiled. "That's not the only difference," he said. Nick asked the driver to take them to the Royal Horse Guards Hotel. When Nick opened the door of the cab, the kids could see that the driver was not sitting on the left side of the car.

The cab driver laughed. "I know what you're thinking," he told the kids. "But it's really you American drivers who sit on the wrong side of the car. And you drive on the wrong side of the road, too."

On the way to the hotel, the cab went past Buckingham Palace.

"That's where the Queen lives!" said Mandy. Everyone looked at the enormous building. It was set in a large park with a high fence around it.

There were guards standing in front of the palace. They were wearing red jackets and tall black hats that were made of fur.

"You can see the Queen on Monday," said the driver. "There will be a big parade with horses and guards and a marching band. The Queen will go from here to the Palace of Westminster in her royal coach."

"Where's the Palace of Westminster?" asked Mandy.

"It's right around the corner!" said Nick. As the cab turned the corner, the kids could see a tall tower. At the top of the tower was the biggest clock that they had ever seen. "That's one of the most famous sights in London," Nick said. "That's the Clock Tower at the Palace of Westminster. Everybody calls that clock 'Big Ben,' " said Nick.

"Why does the Queen have two palaces that are so close together?" asked Kris.

"The Palace of Westminster is for Parliament," said the driver.

"What's Parliament?" asked Kris.

"Parliament in England is like Congress in the U.S.," said the driver. "Our government leaders meet there. In your Congress, you have the Senate and the House of Representatives. In our Parliament, we have the House of Lords and the House of Commons," explained the driver. "On Monday, the Queen will get all dressed up and put on her royal crown. Then she will give a speech to all the members of Parliament."

"That sounds exciting," said Mandy.

Chapter 3

The Clue

Ken looked at the Clock Tower. "Now I can set my watch to match the correct time in London," he said.

"Yes," said Nick. "Big Ben has been telling people the correct time since 1859."

The cab driver spoke. "Not anymore," he said. "Someone killed Big Ben last night." The driver held up a London Times newspaper. Jeff read the headline out loud. The headline said "BIG BEN IS DEAD."

Jeff took the newspaper from the cab driver. There was a picture of Big Ben on the front page. In the picture, the clock showed the same time as it showed now.

"The hands on the clock are stopped at 1 o'clock," said Mandy.

Kris laughed. "At least it will show the correct time twice a day," she said.

"Very funny," said Jeff. "Listen to this." Jeff read from the newspaper. "Early this morning, Big Ben was attacked by thieves. The thieves stole an important gear from the clock.

Without this gear, the hands of the clock will not turn. When the police from Scotland Yard arrived, they found a note. The note may help them find the gear from the clock."

"Why did they have to get the police from Scotland to help on this case?" asked Mandy.

"The police aren't from Scotland," said Nick. "They are from Scotland Yard. Scotland Yard is the name of the police headquarters in London."

"That's right," said the cab driver. "500 years ago there was a palace on that spot. The kings and queens of Scotland used to stay in the palace when they came to London, so people called the palace Scotland Yard. When the police built their headquarters there, they kept the name."

Kris looked at Jeff. "Tell us about the clue," she said.

Jeff kept on reading from the newspaper. "The clue said, 'A stitch in time saves nine.' The clue was signed by 'Mohammed Ali.' "

Ken shouted, "Muhammad Ali? What's he got to do with this? He's a boxer, not a thief!"

"And what does it mean when you say 'a stitch in time saves nine?' " asked Kris.

"Do any of you kids know how to sew?" asked Nick.

"I can sew on a button," said Jeff. "But that's about it."

"Let's say that you get a little hole in your shirt," said Nick. "If you get a needle and thread and you stitch it up right away, it will be easy to fix the hole. You can fix it with just one or two stitches, right?" he asked.

Kris nodded her head, yes.

"But if you wait too long, the hole will get bigger," said Nick. "Then it might take you nine or ten stitches to fix the hole instead of one or two stitches."

"I get it," said Mandy. "A stitch in time, saves nine! But what does that have to do with the clock?"

The driver spoke. "If I knew the answer to that question, I would be a rich man," he said.

"How would that make you rich?" asked Ken.

"Because Scotland Yard is offering a reward to anyone who finds the thieves or the missing gear from the clock," said the driver.

"What is the reward?" asked Ken.

"10,000 pounds," the driver answered.

"That's a lot of money," said Nick. "That's over $15,000."

"Wow," said Ken. "I could pay for college next year with that much money. Maybe we should try to solve this mystery!"

Chapter 4

Sherlock Holmes

"Now wait a minute," said Nick. "I didn't bring you kids to London to get mixed up in a mystery."

"That's true, Dad," said Kris. "But something like this could keep Ken and Jeff awake for a while."

The cab driver spoke. "Everyone in London is looking for the gear that was taken from Big Ben," he said. "They are looking for it for two reasons. First, we English people are proud of our history, and Big Ben is an important part of that history. Second, everyone wants to be a hero!"

The cab came to a stop. "Here you are," said the driver. "This is the Royal Horse Guards Hotel."

Nick paid the driver. Then Nick and the kids went into the hotel. "Let's go to our rooms," he said. "We'll meet back here in 15 minutes. Then we can go and get something to eat."

A man at the hotel told Nick about a good place to have lunch. "It's called the Sherlock Holmes Pub," said the man. "It's just around the corner."

"That sounds like fun," said Jeff. "I love to read Sherlock Holmes mysteries. Sherlock Holmes lived in London a long time ago. He had a friend named Doctor Watson and they solved a lot of crimes here."

"It's too bad that they are not alive now," said Kris. "They could solve the mystery about Big Ben."

"Sherlock Holmes wasn't a real person," said Jeff. "A man named Sir Arthur Conan Doyle made up the stories about Sherlock Holmes."

When Nick and the kids stepped inside the Sherlock Holmes Pub, Jeff got excited. On the walls, there were many pictures from the Sherlock Holmes mystery stories.

A waitress came over to Nick.

"How many are in your group?" she asked.

"There are five of us," said Nick.

"I have one table left upstairs," said the waitress. "It's pretty crowded up there because there's a meeting going on."

"Maybe we should go somewhere else," said Nick.

"Oh no," said the waitress. "You'll enjoy this meeting. It's the Sherlock Holmes Club. The people in the club like to help solve real mysteries and they're trying to solve the mystery of Big Ben!"

"That's great," said Jeff. "Let's check it out!"

Everyone followed Jeff upstairs into a crowded room. Many people were talking there.

Jeff could see that the room had tables and chairs, but it was also set up like a museum. The pictures on the wall were from old Sherlock Holmes movies.

One wall had a huge window. The window let people see into the next room. Jeff pointed at the window. "That room behind the glass is set up just like the room where Sherlock Holmes worked," he said. "Look, the fireplace and the desk look just like the ones in the books.

And there's a microscope on the table and a violin on a chair. Sherlock Holmes played the violin."

Just then another group of people ran up the stairs and into the big room. "We found it!" yelled a woman. "We found the gear for Big Ben!"

Chapter 5

The Needle

Everyone in the pub began to clap as the woman held up a small, round gear. Someone took her picture. An old man stood up. "I say!" said the old man. "Jolly good show!" Then he spoke to the others in the room. "England will be proud of us today!" he said.

"Excuse me," said a man with a camera. "I'm a reporter from the London Times newspaper. Would you mind telling me how you found that gear?"

The old man spoke. "My name is Sir John Sims. I'm the president of the Sherlock Holmes Club. Our club meets here once a week. We solve crimes for a hobby."

Sir John pointed to a large pad of paper. The words of the clue for Big Ben were printed on the paper. "This morning our club had a special meeting to help with the Big Ben case," he said.

Sir John read the clue out loud. "A stitch in time saves nine," he read.

Then Sir John took a marking pen and drew a red circle around the word *time*. "That word means 'Big Ben,' " he said. Then he drew a circle around the name *Mohammed Ali*. "That could be the famous boxer," he said. "But it is also the name of a leader in Egypt who gave a present to the people of England in 1819." Next Sir John drew a circle around the word *stitch*. "You need a needle to make a stitch," he said. "The thief was talking about Cleopatra's Needle. That's the gift that Mohammed Ali gave us in 1819!"

"What's Cleopatra's Needle?" asked Ken.

"Cleopatra's Needle is a stone that was carved in Egypt 3,475 years ago," said Sir John. "The stone is 60 feet tall and it weighs nearly 200 tons! It's just a few blocks from here," said Sir John. "You'd better go and see it before this man from the newspaper writes his story. There will be too many people there tomorrow."

Sir John turned to the woman who was holding the gear. "Did you find anything else?" he asked.

"Yes," said the woman. "We found an envelope." She handed it to Sir John.

Sir John put his glasses on. He opened the envelope. He took a note out of the envelope and began to read it to himself. "I say!" he said at last.

"Will you read it to us?" someone asked.

Sir John began to read the note out loud.

"To the citizens of England:

Big Ben is an important part of

your country. You should protect

it better. If I can make Big Ben

stop ticking, then anyone can

do it.

It will be just as easy for me to

steal other national treasures.

I will show you how easy it is.

'A stitch in time saves nine'

means that I plan to take nine

things. The gear from Big Ben

is just the first one."

Chapter 6

The Painting

The next morning, Nick told the kids that he had to go to the British Museum to meet with the scientists there.

"Why don't you walk to the museum and meet me at 5 o'clock," said Nick.

Kris and Mandy were looking at a map of London. "First, we could stop at the National Gallery," said Mandy. "I'd like to see the famous paintings there. It will be exciting," she said.

Ken looked at Jeff. "What are we getting into here?" Ken asked. "That sounds boring to me."

"We'd better stay with Kris and Mandy," teased Jeff. "They might get lost in the gift shop."

The kids said good-bye to Nick and walked to the museum.

"We can borrow a CD player here for free," said Mandy. "The CD tells about every painting in the museum."

"This place is huge," said Ken. "Do we have to stay here all day?"

Mandy laughed. "No," she said. "We'll just stay for one hour. I promise!"

Mandy took them to a part of the museum called the East Wing. "The paintings in this gallery were painted in the 1800's and 1900's," said Mandy. "You will see famous paintings here by artists like Vincent van Gogh and Pablo Picasso."

Kris pointed to a painting of sunflowers in the first room. "There's a painting by Vincent van Gogh," she said.

Kris and Ken walked over to the painting. Kris read the card on the wall next to it.

"Sunflowers. Vincent van Gogh. 1888," she read. "Now press number 4-9-7 on your CD player, Ken," said Kris. "It will tell you more about the painting."

Ken pushed 4-9-7 on his CD player. A man's voice began to speak.

"Vincent van Gogh finished this painting of 15 sunflowers during the summer of 1888." Ken stopped the CD player. He looked at the painting and counted the sunflowers. Then he called to Kris.

"Hey, Kris," said Ken. "How many sunflowers do you see in this painting?" he asked.

Kris counted the flowers. "I see 13," she said. "Why?"

"Well, the man on the CD says there are 15 sunflowers," said Ken. "So what happened to the other two?"

Ken walked over to a guard by the door of the gallery. "Excuse me, sir," said Ken. "How many flowers are supposed to be in that painting by van Gogh over there?"

"Fifteen," said the guard.

"Well then, something is wrong," said Ken. "You're missing two flowers."

The guard walked over to the painting and looked at it very closely. Then he looked at Ken and Kris. "Stay right where you are," said the guard. He took a walkie-talkie from his belt and spoke into it. "This is Robert in gallery 45," said the guard. "The van Gogh painting of sunflowers has been stolen!"

Chapter 7

The Stretch Limo

In just a few minutes, there were ten more guards in the gallery with Ken and Kris.

Jeff and Mandy had been in the next gallery. When they saw the guards, they rushed back to Ken and Kris.

"What's going on?" asked Jeff.

One of the guards spoke. "We are going to take all of you down to Scotland Yard," he said.

"What did we do?" asked Kris.

"You seem to know something about this fake painting," said the guard. "Someone has stolen a painting that is worth millions."

Ken looked closely at the fake painting. He saw that one of the corners of the painting was bent. "Wait a minute," said Ken. "This painting has been stuck into the old picture frame. I think the real painting is still under there!"

The guard stood next to Ken and looked at the painting again. Then he took out a small pocketknife.

He slid the blade of the knife between the fake painting and the picture frame. When he lifted the knife, the fake painting came out. Ken was right! The real painting was still there!

Ken took the fake painting and turned it over. There was an envelope taped to the back of the painting.

"I'll bet that it's a letter from the thief," said Jeff.

Ken opened the envelope and read the note.

"To the citizens of England:

The paintings in this museum

are an important part of your

country. You should protect

them better.

I could have taken the real

painting if I had wanted to.

This museum needs more

guards."

One of the guards spoke to the

kids. "I'm terribly sorry," he said.

"You are free to go.

I will give this letter to Scotland Yard. It looks as if we have a crazy person on the loose in London," said the guard.

Jeff took the CD players back to the desk. Then he met Mandy, Kris, and Ken outside. "You were right, Mandy," said Jeff. "A museum can be an exciting place."

Kris spoke. "I'm not so sure that the person who is stealing these things is crazy," she said. "I think that we should walk to the British Museum right away.

I want to tell Dad about this before we get stopped by a newspaper reporter."

"I have a better idea," said Mandy. "Let's take a cab."

Ken ran down the steps of the National Gallery. He waved at a cab that was coming toward him. The cab didn't stop, but a big stretch limo pulled up right next to Ken. The windows in the limo were dark. Suddenly, the window next to the driver opened. "I saw you trying to stop that cab," said the driver. "May I give you a lift?"

"My friends and I are going to the British Museum," said Ken.

"Get in," said the driver. "It's right on my way."

Chapter 8

The Man with the Cane

Ken waved at Jeff and Kris and Mandy. "Come on!" yelled Ken. He pointed at the limo. "We're going in style!"

Ken opened the back door of the limo and the kids got in. An old man was sitting in the back seat, looking out the window. He had thick glasses and a beard. He was wearing a top hat and a tuxedo. The man had gloves on his hands and he was holding a shiny black cane with a silver handle. He didn't look at the kids.

When the limo stopped in front of the British Museum, the kids were glad to get out.

"That was weird," said Ken.

"Look at this," said Jeff. He was holding an envelope. "That old man just handed this to me."

Jeff opened the envelope. Inside the envelope was a postcard. The postcard showed a statue of a green cat. The cat had a gold ring in its nose and a gold earring. There was a message on the back of the postcard.

Mandy and Kris and Ken stood next to Jeff and read the message.

Jeff handed the postcard to Kris. Then he ran back to the street and stopped a cab. Ken ran after him.

Mandy yelled at the boys. "Hey! Where are you going?" she asked.

"We're going after that old man in the limo!" Jeff said. "Take that postcard and show it to Nick!"

Mandy and Kris turned back toward the museum. There was a big crowd of people standing by the front door.

A woman was talking to them. "I'm terribly sorry," she said. "The museum is closed for the rest of today. We have an emergency inside!"

Kris and Mandy walked up to a guard at the front door. "Excuse me, sir," said Kris. "My name is Kris Ford. My dad is Nick Ford and he is inside working with some scientists. May we go in and see him?"

"I'm sorry," said the guard. "No one may go in or out. Something has been stolen."

Mandy spoke. "Is it a green cat?" she asked.

The man looked at Mandy in surprise. Then he said, "I will call Mr. Ford right away."

In a few minutes, Nick was standing at the front door with two policemen. Kris could see that Nick was carrying his laptop computer. Kris handed the postcard to her dad. She told him about Jeff and Ken. Nick read the message and said, "Come inside, girls."

Nick led Kris and Mandy to a part of the museum that was filled with artifacts from Egypt. The girls couldn't believe their eyes! They saw mummies and coffins that were made out of stone. And they saw walls with Egyptian writing on them. There were also glass cases with beautiful statues and bowls in them.

Nick and the men stopped by one of the glass cases. Nick tapped the glass on the case. "Take a look at that," he said.

Both girls looked. Instead of a statue or a bowl, they saw a postcard of a green cat.

"It's just like *our* postcard!" said Mandy.

Chapter 9

The Green Cat

Many people who worked at the museum stood next to Nick and the glass case. The people were angry.

A policeman from Scotland Yard spoke to them. "As you all know by now, someone has stolen the most famous cat of ancient Egypt," he said. "We don't know how it was taken. The glass in this case has not been broken."

Nick spoke. "I want to introduce you to my daughter, Kris, and to our friend, Mandy Ming," said Nick.

"I think that the girls may have brought us a clue about the cat."

Kris told everyone about the van Gogh painting of sunflowers. Mandy told them about the limo ride to the British Museum and about the old man in the limo. Nick held up the postcard and read the words on the back of it.

"The rose is black.
The cat is green.
You will need a key
For number three to be seen."

The policeman asked Nick to read the clue again slowly. A few people wrote down the words.

"Does anyone know what this means?" asked the policeman.

Mandy spoke. "The word *three* probably means that the cat is the robber's third target," she said. "Big Ben was the first target and the painting by Vincent van Gogh was the second target."

"The clue says that we will need a key to get the cat back," said the policeman.

"So I want to know about anything in the museum that is locked up with a key. Does anyone else have an idea?" asked the policeman.

No one spoke. Kris took the postcard from Nick and read the clue again.

"The rose is black.

The cat is green.

You will need a key

For number three to be seen."

"I know this sounds stupid," Kris said. "But do you have any black roses in the museum?"

No one knew.

"Maybe we are thinking about the wrong kind of key," said Mandy. "Maybe the key in the clue doesn't unlock a door at all," she said. "Maybe the key unlocks a mystery!"

Nick spoke. "You just gave me an idea, Mandy," he said. Nick took out his laptop computer and opened it. Everyone watched as Nick put a CD in the computer and turned it on.

Chapter 10

The Stray Cat

Kris looked at Nick. "Why are you putting that CD in your computer?" she asked.

"This CD has a list of every artifact in the British Museum," said Nick. "I'm going to type in the word 'rose' and see if there is a black rose anywhere in the British Museum."

People crowded around Nick to look at his computer. Nick began to type the letters. R...O... Nick saw the words ROMAN COINS appear on the list. Nick typed the next letter.

R...O...S...   Now Nick saw the words ROSETTA STONE.

A cheer went up from the people. "By George, he's got it!" yelled a man. "The black rose must mean the Rosetta Stone."

"Good show!" shouted another man.

"Hello?" said Kris. "Would someone like to tell me about the Rosetta Stone?" she asked. "That doesn't sound like a black rose to me!"

Mandy laughed. "You should have taken my ancient history class," said Mandy. "The Rosetta Stone is a huge black rock from Egypt. It has words on it," she said. "The same words are written in three different languages. One of the languages is Greek and the other two languages are Egyptian. One of the Egyptian languages uses pictures for words. The writing is called 'hieroglyphics.'" Mandy pointed to a wall nearby. "See the picture writing on that wall over there?" she said.

"No one knew what those hieroglyphics meant until the Rosetta Stone was found. The Rosetta Stone was the key that unlocked the mystery of the hieroglyphics!"

"You're right, Mandy," said Nick. "The Rosetta Stone is a key that unlocks a mystery! Let's go have a look at it."

When they got near the stone, Mandy spoke to Kris. "I knew about the Rosetta Stone," she said. "But I didn't know that it was so big!"

The stone was the size of a desk. It was sitting on a metal stand.

Nick and the director of the museum walked behind the stone. There on the floor was the lost green cat! It was sitting on an envelope.

Nick smiled. "There seems to be a stray cat back here," he said. "Did anyone lose a cat?" Everyone cheered.

The director put on a pair of gloves. Then he picked up the cat.

Nick teased the man. "Are you afraid that it will scratch you?" he asked.

The director laughed. "No," he said. "If I didn't wear gloves, the oil from my hands would leave fingerprints on the metal."

Nick looked at the cat carefully as the director picked it up. "I think that the thief must have been wearing gloves, also, because I don't see any fingerprints on the cat," said Nick. He picked up the envelope and opened it. He took out a note.

"What does it say?" asked Kris.

Nick read the note to himself. Then he read it out loud.

"To the citizens of England: The artifacts in the British Museum belong to the people of the world. You should protect them better.
I could have taken the cat right out the front door and kept it. You should keep your cat on a leash."

Chapter 11

The Chase

While Nick and the girls were in the museum, Ken and Jeff were in a cab. "Follow that white limo!" Ken yelled at the driver. "The Big Ben thief may be in that car!"

Jeff and Ken could hear the tires of the cab squeal as the driver turned a corner. The driver looked in the rear view mirror at the boys. "Put on your seat belts, mates!" yelled the driver.

The limo was more than two blocks ahead of the cab. The limo turned left into an alley. But when the cab turned into the same alley, the limo was gone.

"We've lost them!" yelled Jeff.

The driver put the cab into reverse and stepped on the gas. The cab shot back out of the alley and spun around.

The driver pointed at a street across a park. "There's the limo!" he shouted. "It's on the next street!"

"How do we get over there from here?" asked Ken.

The cab driver did not answer. He aimed the cab at the park and stepped on the gas. There was a big BANG as the cab hit the curb by the sidewalk.

Ken could feel the cab leave the ground and fly through the air. It landed on the lawn inside the park.

"We're headed for that lake!" Ken yelled.

Jeff could feel the car skid as the driver steered away from the lake. Suddenly, he saw two black swans fly up into the air. Ken was sure that the swans would crash into the front window of the cab. He closed his eyes and listened, but there was no crash. Ken slowly opened his eyes.

The swans were gone, but the front window of the cab was covered with mud and water.

The boys felt another BANG as the cab crossed the sidewalk on the other side of the park. The driver turned the car sharply back onto the street. Ken and Jeff could see that the white limo was only a block away now.

"Don't get too close," said Jeff. "We don't want them to know that we're following them."

The cab followed the limo for more than 25 miles. They were out in the countryside now. They drove through hills that were covered with trees and green fields.

"Where are we?" asked Jeff.

"This is Windsor, mate," said the driver. "The Queen has another castle near here. Your friend in that limo must have a house next door to the Queen."

The boys watched the limo slow down. It turned into a driveway and waited for a large gate to open.

Then the limo went through the gate and disappeared among the trees. The gate closed behind the limo.

"We'll get out here," said Jeff. "How much do we owe you?"

"I don't know yet," said the driver. "I'm going to sit right here and wait for you, mates," he said. "There may be trouble behind that gate."

Chapter 12

The Black Cane

Ken and Jeff waited until it was nearly dark. Then they climbed over the fence. The main house was about a mile down the driveway.

The boys walked to the house and hid behind a large fountain.

"Look at the size of this place!" said Ken. "It must have a hundred rooms."

"Yes," said Jeff. "But right now I only see one light on. Let's check it out."

Ken and Jeff walked carefully toward the light in the window. They could hear voices inside.

"Tonight we will get the biggest prize of all," said a voice. "Tonight we will steal the Queen's crown!"

"That's impossible, Sir John!" said another voice. "The crown is locked up in the Tower of London with all of the other Crown Jewels. No one can get into the Tower!"

"You're right!" said the first voice. "But tomorrow the Queen will give a speech to the members of Parliament. She must wear her crown for that speech.

That means that right now someone is supposed to take the crown from the Tower of London to Buckingham Palace. But that person isn't *taking* the crown," said the first voice. "He's *stealing* the crown!"

Ken and Jeff could hear men laughing. Ken stood up slowly and peeked into the window. Then he quickly sat back down next to Jeff.

"You're not going to believe this," whispered Ken.

"What?" asked Jeff.

"We have seen those men before," said Ken. "They are all members of the Sherlock Holmes Club! That's Sir John Sims, the president of the club! The old man in the limo today was Sir John!"

"How do you know that it was Sir John?" asked Jeff.

"See for yourself," said Ken. "Look at the things that are on the table. There's a fake beard, a top hat, a pair of gloves, and a black cane with a silver handle!"

Jeff stood up and looked at the table. He looked at the men in the room. They were all wearing tuxedos. They looked very rich. Jeff sat back down.

The boys could hear one of the men speaking to Sir John. "Maybe this time people will really pay attention," said the man. "Maybe now they will see how important it is to protect our national treasures."

"Who is going to steal the crown?" asked another man.

"I have hired Patrick Farley to do it,"
said Sir John. "He is the most famous
thief in England. He's pretending to
be a guard. He will get the crown
from the Tower, but he won't take it
to Buckingham Palace."

"What will happen if Mr. Farley does
not give back the crown?" asked one
of the men.

"Now there's a sticky wicket!" said
Sir John.

Jeff and Ken went back to the cab.
The driver was still waiting.

He rolled down his window. "Where to, mates?" he asked.

"Take us to Buckingham Palace," said Jeff. "We need to see the Queen."

Chapter 13

The Queen

The next morning, Nick and the kids ate breakfast at the hotel.

Kris looked at Jeff and Ken. "So you went to see the Queen last night," said Kris. "Did the Queen serve you tea?"

"That's not even funny," said Jeff. "The guards wouldn't let us past the front gate."

Nick spoke. "But you did give the guards the message about Sir John Sims," said Nick. "That's the important part."

"But what if they didn't give the message to the Queen?" asked Ken.

Nick stood up. "The guards gave your message to the right person all right," he said. Nick started to leave.

"Where are you going, Dad?" asked Kris. "I haven't finished my breakfast yet."

"I'll be right back," Nick answered. "You kids just wait right there."

In a few minutes, Nick returned to the table. He had two other men with him. One of the men was dressed in a red and black uniform.

Nick spoke to the kids. "I would like you to meet Inspector Penn from Scotland Yard," he said. "And this is Tony Martin. Tony is a Beefeater at the Tower of London."

"I love to eat beef," said Ken. "That sounds like my kind of job!"

Tony laughed. "A 'Beefeater' is a guard at the Tower of London," he said.

"The Tower is one of the Queen's palaces. She keeps the Crown Jewels there," explained Tony. "The Queen will be wearing her crown in Parliament today and it's all because of you two boys."

Inspector Penn held up five tickets. "Yes," he said. "We thought that you might like to see the Queen for yourselves. So here are five tickets for the Opening of Parliament today. The Queen will be speaking in the House of Lords, and you're invited!"

"Thank you so much!" said Mandy.

"And I have something else for each of you," said the Inspector. He handed them each an envelope.

"What's this?" asked Ken.

"It's the reward money," said the Inspector. "You all get to share the reward for helping us solve this case."

Nick smiled. "I'm proud of you, also," he said. Then Nick asked Inspector Penn a question. "What about Sir John Sims?" he asked. "Will he go to prison?"

"Sir John is a member of the House of Lords in Parliament," said Inspector Penn. "Sir John loves England and he wanted to warn us that our national treasures are in danger."

"Yes," said Tony. "Sir John took some important things, but he gave everything back. He is a very rich man."

"This morning Sir John gave us something else, also," said Inspector Penn.

"Sir John gave Scotland Yard a check for five million pounds to start a new program. This program will make our treasures safer."

Tony and the inspector walked with Nick and the kids to the House of Parliament. They watched the Queen's parade along the way.

"Check out Big Ben," said Jeff. "It has the right time!"

Inspector Penn gave the tickets to a guard at Parliament and the guard took Nick and the kids to their seats.

When the Queen arrived, Ken and Jeff were happy to see that she was wearing her crown.

The Queen walked to her throne and began to speak. "My Lords and Members of the House of Commons," said the Queen. " My government shall always fight against crime. During the past week, my government saw a new kind of crime in England. Someone took our finest treasures, and then gave them back to us! This person was trying to warn us that our national treasures are in danger."

The Queen looked over at Nick and the kids and smiled. "My Lords and Members of the House," she said. "My government shall do its part to protect our treasures."

Everyone cheered.

Ken and Jeff looked around the room at all the members of Parliament. There was Sir John Sims! When he saw the boys looking at him, he reached inside his jacket and took out an envelope. Then he smiled.

The End

About the Writer

Jerry Stemach is a Special Educator who has worked with middle and high school students and adults learning English as a second language for more than 25 years. He has served students with language and learning disabilities as a Speech and Language Pathologist, an assistive technology specialist, and as a Special Education teacher.

Jerry is a member of the Start-to-Finish editing team. For the Nick Ford series, he personally visits each city, state, or country that he writes about so that he can tell the story with interesting facts.

Jerry makes his home in the Valley of the Moon in Sonoma County, California with his wife, Beverly, and daughters, Sarah and Kristie.

About the Reader

Ed Smaron was born in Chicago and now lives in Los Angeles. He has acted in plays in the theater, and he has performed in TV commercials. You can also hear Ed's voice in many video games including *Resident Evil* and a new game called *Dead to Rights*. Ed played a leading role in the film *Borderland*.

Ed plays music, too. He has gone on tour as the musical director of a famous comedy group from Chicago called Second City.

If you have read any of the *Nick Ford Mysteries* or *Classic Adventures* from Start-to-Finish, then you have already heard the wonderful voice of Ed Smaron.

A Note from the Start-to-Finish™ Editors

This book has been divided into approximately equal short chapters so that the student can read a chapter and take the cloze test in one reading session. This length constraint has sometimes required the authors and editors to make transitions in mid-chapter or to break up chapters in unexpected places.

You will also notice that Start-to-Finish™ Books look different from other high-low readers and chapter books. The text layout of this book coordinates with the other media components (CD and audiocassette) of the Start-to-Finish™ series.

The text in the book matches, line for line and page for page, the text shown on the computer screen, enabling readers to follow along easily in the book. Each page ends in a complete sentence so that the student can either practice the page (repeat reading) or turn the page to continue with the story. If the next sentence cannot fit on the page in its entirety, it has been shifted to the next page. For this reason, the sentence at the top of a page may not be indented, signaling that it is part of the paragraph from the preceding page.

Words are not hyphenated at the ends of lines. This sometimes creates extra space at the end of a line, but eliminates confusion for the struggling reader.